For my parents, for everything—A. B.

For Ariel Bernstein—S. M.

SIMON & SCHUSTER BOOKS FOR YOUNG READERS
An imprint of Simon & Schuster Children's Publishing Division
1230 Avenue of the Americas, New York, New York 10020
Text copyright © 2019 by Ariel Bernstein
Illustrations copyright © 2019 by Scott Magoon

For information about special discounts for bulk purchases, please contact Simon & Schuster Special Sales at 1-866-506-1949 or business@simonandschuster.com.
The Simon & Schuster Speakers Bureau can bring authors to your live event. For more information or to book an event,
contact the Simon & Schuster Speakers Bureau at 1-866-248-3049 or visit our website at www.simonspeakers.com.
Book design by Chloë Foglia • The text for this book was set in Geometric 415. • The illustrations for this book were rendered digitally.
Manufactured in China • 1118 SCP • First Edition
2 4 6 8 10 9 7 5 3 1
Library of Congress Cataloging-in-Publication Data
Names: Bernstein, Ariel, author. | Magoon, Scott, illustrator. Title: Where is my balloon? / written by Ariel Bernstein ; illustrated by Scott Magoon.
Description: First edition. | New York : Simon & Schuster Books for Young Readers, [2019] | Summary: While holding his friend
Owl's red balloon, Monkey accidentally pops it then tries to substitute other objects before confessing his deed.
Identifiers: LCCN 2018000334 | ISBN 9781534414518 (hardcover) | ISBN 9781534414525 (eBook)
Subjects: | CYAC: Balloons—Fiction. | Accidents—Fiction. | Friendship—Fiction. | Owls—Fiction. | Monkeys—
Fiction. | Humorous stories. | Classification: LCC PZ7.1.B463 Whe 2019 | DDC [E]—dc23
LC record available at https://lccn.loc.gov/2018000334

WHERE IS MY BALLOON?

Written by Ariel Bernstein

Illustrated by Scott Magoon

A Paula Wiseman Book
Simon & Schuster Books for Young Readers
New York   London   Toronto   Sydney   New Delhi

I have a balloon.

I have a sock.

Please hold my balloon.
I will be right back.

I have a sock.
AND I have a balloon!
This makes me SO HAPPY!

I can put my sock
over the balloon.

I can tie my sock to the balloon string.

I can hit the balloon with my sock like it's a baseball.

Uh-oh.

Hello, Monkey. I am back.
May I please have my balloon?

Your balloon?

Yes, my balloon.

A balloon? Hmmm. Please
hold my sock while I check.

Here is your balloon.

Monkey, this is not my balloon.

I'm pretty sure it's a balloon.

This is *not* a balloon.
This is a pillow.
An orange pillow.
My balloon is red.

I'll be right back.

Here is your red balloon.

This is not my balloon. This is a red chair.
My balloon is **big** and **red**.

I can't believe it.
I'll be right back.

Here is your **big** red balloon.

This is big and red. But this is not my balloon. This is a fire truck.

This is a fire truck? Are you sure?

This is a fire truck. This is really, truly a fire truck. My balloon is **big** and **red** and **flies** in the **air!**

Here is your **big red** balloon
that **flies** in the **air**.

This is big, red, and flies in the air.
But this is a parachute, Monkey.
Where is my balloon?

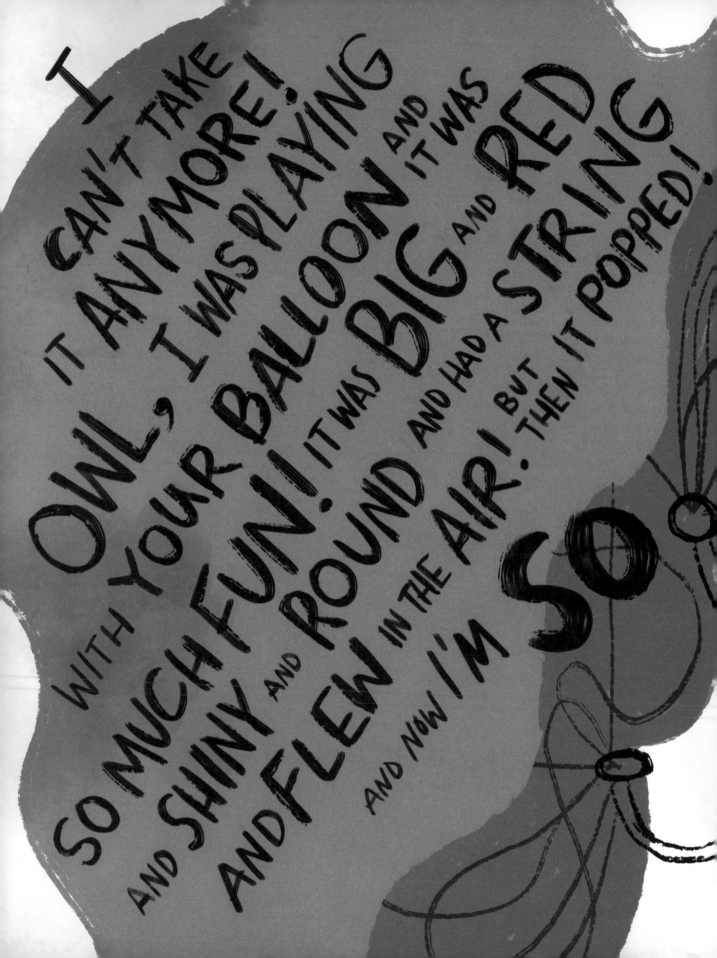

I CAN'T TAKE IT ANYMORE! I WAS PLAYING WITH YOUR BALLOON AND IT WAS SO MUCH FUN!! IT WAS BIG AND RED AND SHINY AND ROUND AND HAD A STRING AND FLEW IN THE AIR. BUT THEN IT POPPED! AND NOW I'M SO

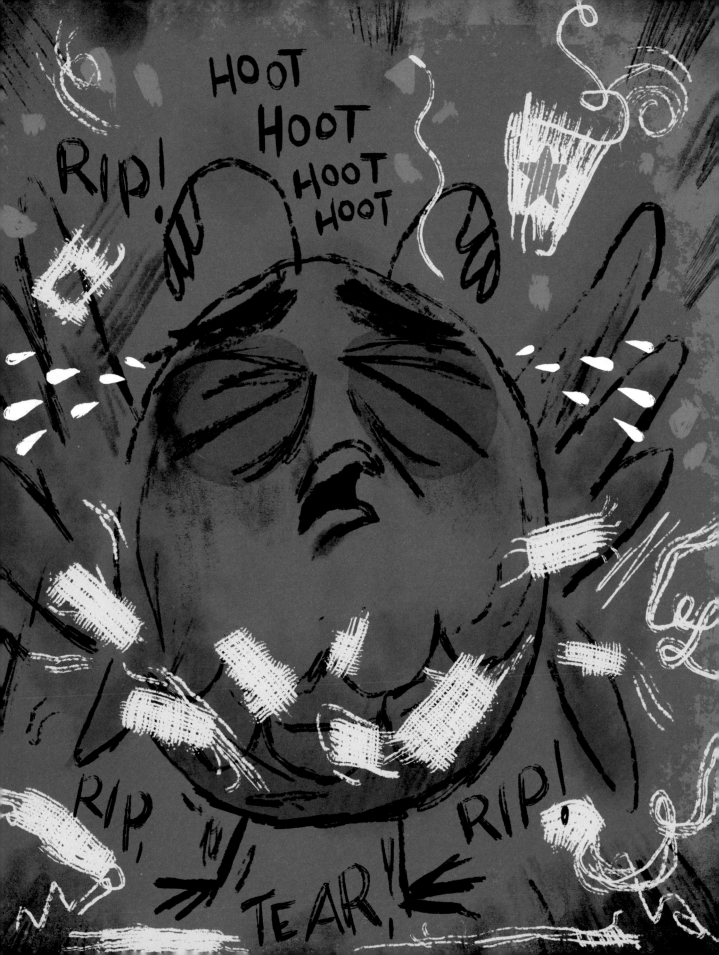

I am sad to lose my balloon, Monkey. But I forgive you.

Thank you, Owl.

We can play together
with my sock.

Your **sock?**

Yes.
My **sock** with a **star**
and a
**perfectly
shaped hole.**

I will be right back.

This is your sock.